DISCARDED

Jorinda and Joringel

by the Brothers Grimm

Illustrated by Bernadette

The World Publishing Company / New York and Cleveland

Published by The World Publishing Company
110 East 59th Street, New York, New York 10022
Library of Congress catalog card number: 71-114218
Text and illustrations copyright © 1970 by Nord-Süd Verlag, Switzerland
All rights reserved. No part of this book may be reproduced
in any form without written permission from the publisher, except for
brief passages included in a review appearing in a newspaper or magazine.
First published in Switzerland in 1970 by Nord-Süd Verlag, Switzerland
Published in England in 1970 by Oxford University Press, London.

For Arabella and Johnny

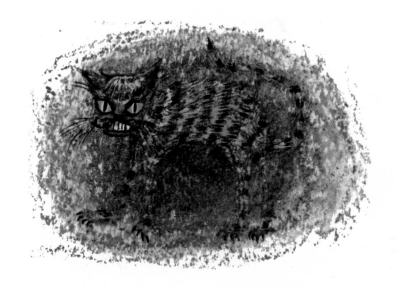

There was once an old castle in the middle of a vast, thick forest. In it there lived an old woman all alone. She was a witch. By day she took the shape of a cat or an owl, and at night she became a human being again. She knew how to lure wild creatures to her with magic spells, and she would roast them and eat them.

If a man came within a hundred paces of the castle, he was rooted to the spot, and could not move until the witch set him free. But if a young girl came near, the witch changed her into a bird, shut her up in a cage, and carried the cage into a room in the castle. There must have been seven thousand cages in the castle, each with a pretty bird in it.

Now there was once a maiden called Jorinda, who was more beautiful than any
other maiden. She had a sweetheart called Joringel. Jorinda and Joringel loved each
other dearly and longed to be married. One day they wandered into the forest so

that they could be alone together. "We must take care not to go too near the castle,"
said Joringel.

It was a beautiful evening. The sun glanced brightly through the tree trunks in the dark greenwood, and the turtledoves cooed plaintively in the old beech trees. Jorinda and Joringel sat down to enjoy the sunshine, but for some reason they were both sad. They had a feeling that soon they would be parted forever.

They had come a long way. When the sun had sunk halfway below the top of the mountain, they rose to go home; but they could not find the path. Joringel peered through the thicket, looking for it, and suddenly he saw the castle walls ahead of him. He cried out and turned pale. Without knowing it, they had been sitting quite close to the castle.

Jorinda was singing softly:

> "My little bird with its ring so red
> Sings sorrow, sorrow, sorrow:
> My little bird sings of when I am dead,
> Sings sorrow, sorr—"

Suddenly the song stopped.

Jorinda had turned into a nightingale, and now she sang sadly "Jug, jug, jug!" An owl with burning eyes flew three times around her, and three times screeched "Shu-shu-hu-hu!" And before Joringel could catch hold of the nightingale and carry it away, he was himself bewitched. He stood there like a stone, unable to move. He could not speak, he could not cry out, he could not move hand or foot. Then the owl seized the nightingale and flew off into the thicket.

The sun had set, and now the witch came out of the thicket, carrying the nightingale. Her face was green and she had angry red eyes and a long hooked nose that reached to her pointed chin. She muttered something and disappeared into the castle, taking the nightingale with her. Joringel was heartbroken to see the nightingale taken away.

At last the witch came back and said in a hollow voice: "Greetings to thee, Zachiel! When the moon shines on the cage, Zachiel, set the captive free."

Then Joringel was free. He fell down on his knees before the witch and begged her to give him back his Jorinda, but the old woman cackled and said he should never have her again. At that, she vanished into the forest. Joringel wept and lamented, but all in vain. He flung himself down on the grass and cried: "What is to become of me without Jorinda?"

Early the next morning Joringel rose and made his way out of the forest. He came to a strange village, and there he lived for a long time as a shepherd. He often returned to the forest and wandered about near the castle, but he did not go too close. He longed to be near Jorinda, even to hear her singing "Jug, jug, jug!"

One night he dreamed that he found a strange red flower, with a large pearl in the center. In his dream he plucked the flower and took it to the castle. Everything he touched with the flower was freed from the witch's spell, and by means of the red flower he rescued his Jorinda.

In the morning when he awoke Joringel set out to look for the flower. He roamed over hill and dale, searching and searching, and on the ninth day he found the strange red flower. In the center shone a dewdrop as big as the finest pearl. He picked the flower and carried it day and night till he reached the castle.

Joringel came within a hundred paces of the castle, but this time he was not held fast by a spell. He walked straight up to the door and touched it with the flower. It flew open. Joringel was filled with joy. He went in through the courtyard and listened. At last he heard a soft twittering noise. He followed the sound to the room where it came from and stepped inside, with the flower in his upraised hand.

The witch was feeding the birds in their seven thousand cages. When she saw Joringel she was furious. She screamed and raged and tried to catch hold of him, but she could not come near him, for the flower protected him.

Joringel was not concerned about the witch. He was looking among the birdcages. There were hundreds of nightingales! How would he ever find his Jorinda?

While he was wondering what to do, Joringel noticed that the witch had quietly picked up one of the cages and was stealing toward the door.

Joringel leaped in front of the witch and touched her with the flower. She stood as if rooted to the spot. Now her magic had no power.

Then Joringel touched the cage with his flower. The door sprang open, the nightingale flew out, and there in front of him stood his Jorinda. She was as lovely as ever, and she threw her arms joyfully about his neck.

Then Joringel touched all the other cages with his flower, and freed the maidens who had been bewitched.

Joyfully Joringel took his Jorinda by the hand and led her home . . .

. . . and they lived long and happily together.